THE FATAL MARKSMAN

BY

JOHANN AUGUST APEL

Copyright © 2013 Read Books Ltd.

This book is copyright and may not be
reproduced or copied in any way without
the express permission of the publisher in writing

British Library Cataloguing-in-Publication Data
A catalogue record for this book is available from the
British Library

CONTENTS

JOHANN AUGUST APEL 1

THE FATAL MARKSMAN 3

JOHANN AUGUST APEL

Johann August Apel was born in Leipzig, Germany in 1771. He worked as a lawyer and librarian in his hometown for most of his life, and was a keen writer of both classical and speculative fiction. Between 1810 and 1817, in partnership with fellow author F. A. Schulze, he published a large anthology of ghost stories called *Das Gespensterbuch (The Ghost Book)*. This collection included one of his better-known tales, 'The Fatal Marksman'. It also contained 'Die Jägerbraut' ('The Bride Hunter'), which formed the basis for the libretto of *Der Freischütz (The Freeshooter)*, widely regarded as the first important German Romantic opera. Apel died in Leipzig in 1816, aged 44.

THE FATAL MARKSMAN

Johann August Apel

'Listen, dame,' said Bertram, the old forester of Linden to his wife, 'once for all, listen: it's not many things that I would deny to thy asking; but for this notion, Anne, drive it out of thy head – root and branch, the sooner the better; and never encourage the lass to think more about it. When she knows the worst, she submits; and all goes right. I see no good that comes of standing shilly shally, and letting the girl nurse herself with hopes of what must not be.'

'But, Bertram, dear Bertram,' replied old Anne, 'why not? could not our Kate live as happily with the bailiff's clerk as with the hunter Robert? Ah! you don't know what a fine lad William is; so good, so kind-hearted –'

'Like enough,' interrupted Bertram; 'kind-hearted, I dare say, but no hunter for all that. Now look here, Anne: for better than two hundred years has this farm in the forest of Linden come down from father to child in my family. Hadst thou brought me a son, well and good; the farm would have gone to him; and the lass might have married whom she would.

But, as the case stands, – no, I say. It's not altogether Robert that I care about. I don't stand upon trifles; and, if the man is not to your or the girl's, why not look out any other active huntsman that may take my office betimes, and give us a comfortable fireside in our old-age: Robert, or not Robert, so that it be a lad of the forest.'

For the clerk's sake old Anne would have ventured to wheedle her husband a little longer: but the forester, who knew by experience the efficacy of female eloquence, was resolved not to expose his own firmness of purpose to any further assaults or trials; and taking down his gun from the wall, he walked out into the forest.

Scarcely had he turned the corner of the house, when a rosy, light-haired face looked in at the door. It was Katharine: smiling and blushing, she stopped for a moment in agitation, and said, 'Have you succeeded, mother? was it "yes", dear mother?' – Then, bounding into the room, she fell on her mother's neck for an answer.

'Ah, Kate, be not too confident when thou shouldst be prepared for the worst. Thy father is a good man, as good as ever stepped, but he has his fancies; and he is resolved to give thee to none but a hunter: he has set his heart upon it; and he'll not go from his word; I know him too well.'

Katharine wept, and avowed her determination to die sooner than to part from her William. Her mother comforted and scolded her by turns, and at length ended by joining her tears to.her daughter's. She was promising to make one more assault on the old forester's heart, when a knock was heard at the door – and in stepped William. – 'Ah, William!' exclaimed Katharine, with streaming eyes – 'we must part: seek some other sweetheart: me you must never marry; father is resolved to give me to Robert, because he is a huntsman. But, if I am to part from you, to my dying day, dear William, I will remain faithful to you.'

The bursts of wounded feeling were softened in the report of the mother: she exclaimed to the bewildered William, who knew not what to make of Katharine's ejaculations, that Bertram had no objections to him personally; but that, simply, with a view to the reversionary interest in his place as forester, he insisted on having a son-in-law who understood hunting.

'Is that all?' said William, recovering his composure, and at the same time he caught the sobbing girl to his bosom. – 'Is that all? Then be of good cheer, dearest Kate. I am not unskilled in hunting; for at one time I was apprenticed to my uncle Finsterbusch, the forester-general; and it was only to gratify my godfather, the bailiff, that I exchanged the gun for the writing-desk. What care I for the reversion of the bailiff's place, unless I might take my Kate into the bailiff's house as mistress? If you can be content to look no higher than your mother did, and Will the forester is not less dear to you than Will the bailiff, then let me die if I won't quit my clerkship in an instant.'

'Oh! thou dear kind lad,' said Katharine, whilst the clouds dispersed from her fair forehead, and her eyes swam in a shower of glittering tears, 'if thou wilt do this for my sake, then do so, and speak to my father without delay – before he can make any promise to Robert.'

'Stay, Kate; I'll go after him this moment. He's gone to the forest in search of the venison, that is to be delivered tomorrow into the office. Give me a gun and a pouch: I'll meet him with a jolly salutation – and offer my services to him as his hunting-boy.'

The mother and the daughter fell upon his neck; helped to equip him to the best of their skill; and looked after him, as he disappeared in the forest, with hope, but yet with some anxiety.

'This William's a fine fellow!' exclaimed the forester, as he returned home from the chase: 'who would have looked for such a good shot in the flourisher of a crow-quill? Well: tomorrow I shall speak with the bailiff myself: for it would be a sad pity if he were not to pursue the noble profession of hunting. Why, he'll make a second Kuno. You know who Kuno was, I suppose?' said he, turning to William.

William acknowledged that he did not.

'Not know who Kuno was! bless my soul! to think that I should never have told you that? Why, Kuno, you're to understand, was my great grandfather's father; and was the very first man that ever occupied and cultivated this farm. He began the world no better, I'll assure you, than a poor riding boy; and lived servant with the young knight of Wippach. Well, once it happened that this young gentleman of Wippach was present with many other knights and nobles at a great hunt held by the duke. And in this hunt the dogs turned up a stag, upon which a man was seated wringing his hands and crying piteously: for, in those days, there was a tyrannical custom among the great lords, that, when a poor man had committed any slight matter of trespass against the forest-laws, they would take and bind him on the back of a stag, so that he was bruised and gored to death by the herd: or, if he escaped dying that way, he perished of hunger and thirst. Well, when the duke saw this – oh lord! but he was angry; and gave command to stop the hunting; and then and there he promised a high reward to any man that would undertake to hit the stag; but threatened him with the severest displeasure in case he wounded the man; for he was resolved, if possible, to take him alive, that he might learn who it was that had been bold enough to break his law. Now, amongst all the nobility, not a man could be found that would undertake the job on these terms: they liked the reward, mind you, but not the risk. So, at last, who should step forward but Kuno, my own great grandfather's father – the very man that you see painted in that picture. He spoke boldly to the duke, and said, "My noble liege, if it is your pleasure, with God's blessing, I will run the hazard: if I miss, my life is at your grace's disposal, and must pay the forfeit; for riches and worldly goods I have none to ransom it; but I pity the poor man, and, without fee or reward, I would have exposed my life to the same hazard, if I had seen him in the hands of robbers." This speech pleased the duke; it pleased him right well; and he bade Kuno try his luck; and again he promised him the reward in case he hit; but did not repeat his threat in case he missed. Kuno took his gun; cocked it in God's name; and, commending the ball with a pious prayer to the guidance of good angels, spent no time in taking aim, but fired, with a cheerful faith, right into the midst of the thicket; the same moment out rushed the hart, staggered, and fell; the man was unwounded, except that his hands and face were somewhat scratched by the bushes.

'The noble duke kept his word, and gave Kuno, as his reward the farm of the forest to himself and his heirs for ever. But, lord bless us! good fortune never wanted envy; and the favour of Providence, as Kuno soon learned, is followed by the jealousy of man. Many a man there was, in those days, who would gladly have had Kuno's reward; and what did they do but persuade the duke that Kuno's shot has hit the mark through witchcraft and black arts: "For", says he, "Kuno never took any aim, but fired at random – a devil's shot; and a devil's shot, you are to understand, never fails of hitting the mark, for needs must that the devil drives." So hereupon a regulation was made, and from this the custom came, that every descendant of Kuno must undergo a trial, and fire what they call his probational shot, before he is admitted tenant.'

William, who had listened to this story with lively interest, rose from his seat when it was ended, pressed the old man's hand, and promised, under his tuition, to make himself a huntsman such as even old father Kuno should have had no cause to blush for. William had scarcely lived a whole fortnight in his capacity of huntsman, when old Bertram, who liked him better every day, gave a formal consent to his marriage with Katharine. This promise, however, was to be kept secret until the day of the probationary shot. Meantime the bridegroom elect passed his time in rapturous elevation of spirits, and forgot himself and all the world in the paradise of youthful love. – The fact, however, was, that, from that very day, William had met with an unaccountable run of ill-luck in hunting. Sometimes his gun would miss fire; at other times, instead of a deer, he would hit the trunk of a tree. His hunting-bag contained, instead of partridges, daws and crows, and instead of a hare, perhaps a dead cat. At last the forester began to reproach him in good earnest for his heedlessness; and Kate herself became anxious for the event of his examination.

William redoubled his attention and diligence; but, the nearer the day of trial advanced, so much the more was he persecuted by his bad luck. Nearly every shot missed; and at length he grew almost afraid of pulling a trigger, for fear of doing some mischief; for he had already hit a cow at pasture, and narrowly escaped wounding the herdsman.

The Fatal Marksman

'I stick to my own opinion,' said the huntsman one night, 'somebody has cast a spell over William; for in the regular course of nature such things could never happen; and the spell he must undo before he'll have any luck.'

'Take my word for it, William,' said Rudolph, 'it is just what I tell you. Go some Friday at midnight to a cross-road, and make a circle round about you with a ramrod or a bloody sword; bless it three times in the same words the priest uses, but in the name of Samiel –'

'Hush!' interrupted the forester angrily: 'dost know what that name is? he's one of Satan's host. God keep thee and all christians out of his power!'

William crossed himself, and would hear no more; Rudolph persisted in his opinion. All night long he continued to clean his gun, to examine the screws, the spring, and every part of the lock and barrel; and at break of day, he sallied forth to try his luck once more. But all in vain: the deer flocked round him, almost, as it seemed in mockery of his skill. At ten paces distance he levelled at a buck; twice his gun flashed in the pan; the third time the deer darted off unhurt through the bushes. Cursing his fate, the unhappy hunter threw himself despondingly beneath a tree; at that moment a rustling was heard in the bushes, and out limped an old soldier with a wooden leg.

'Good morning to you, comrade,' said the soldier, 'why so gloomy, why so gloomy? Is it body or purse that's ailing, health or wealth is it that you're sighing for? Or has somebody put a charm upon your gun? Come, give us a bit of tobacco; and let's have a little chat together.'

With a surly air William gave him what he asked for, and the soldier threw himself by his side on the grass. The conversation fell on hunting, and William related his own bad luck.

'Let me see your gun,' said the soldier. 'Ah, I thought so: this gun has been charmed, and you'll never get a true aim with it again: and more than that, let me tell you, if the charm was laid according to the rules of art, you'll have no better luck with any other gun you take in hand.'

William shuddered, and would have urged some objection against witchcraft; but the stranger offered to bring the question to a simple test. 'To old soldiers, the like of me,' said he, 'there's nothing at all surprising in it. Bless your soul; I could tell you stories stranger by half, from this time till midnight. Now, here, for instance, is a ball that cannot fail to go true, because it's a gifted ball, and is proof against all the arts of darkness. Just try it now: just give it a trial. I'll answer for it.'

William loaded his piece, and looked about for an aim. At a great height above the forest, like a moving speck, was hovering a large bird of prey. 'There! that old devil, there, shoot him.' William laughed, for the bird was floating in a region so elevated as to be scarcely discernible to the naked eye. 'Nay, never doubt,' repeated the old soldier. 'I'll wager my wooden leg you'll bring him down.' William fired, the black speck was seen rapidly descending; and a great vulture fell bleeding to the ground.

'Oh! that's nothing at all,' said the soldier, observing the speechless astonishment of his companion, 'not worth speaking of. It's no great matter to learn to cast balls as good as these: little more is wanted than some slight matter of skill, and a stout heart: for the work must be done in the night. Meantime here's a few braces of my balls for you,' and so saying he limped off. Filled with astonishment William tried a second of the balls, and again he hit an object at an otherwise inaccessible distance: he then charged with his ordinary balls, and missed the broadest and most obvious mark. On the second trial, he determined to go after the soldier; but he had disappeared in the depths of the forest; all was pleasure when William returned, as formerly, with a load of venison, and gave practical evidence to old Bertram that he was still the same marksman he had shown himself in his noviciate. He should now have told the reason of his late ill-luck, and what course he had taken to remove it; but, without exactly knowing why, he shrank from telling of the inevitable balls, and laid the blame upon a flaw in his gun, which had escaped his notice until the preceding night.

'Now, dame,' said the forester, 'who's wrong now, dame, I wonder? the witchcraft lay in the gun that wanted trimming; and the little devil, that by your account should have thrown down old father Kuno's picture so early this morning, I'm partly of opinion lies in a cankered nail.'

The Fatal Marksman

'What's that about a devil?' asked William.

'Nay, nothing but nonsense,' replied the old man: 'this morning just as the clock was striking seven, the picture fell down of itself; and so my wife will have that all is not right about the house.'

'Just as it was striking seven? Ha!' And the old soldier flashed across William's thoughts, who had taken his leave at the identical time.

In a few days William had so familiarized himself to the use of the enchanted balls, that he no longer regarded them with any misgiving. Every day he roamed about in the forest, hoping to meet the wooden-leg again; for his stock of balls had sunk to a single pair: and the most rigorous parsimony became needful, if he would not put to hazard his final success on the day of trial. One day, therefore, he positively refused attending the old forester a hunting; for, on the next day, the duke's commissioner was expected; and it might so happen that, before the regular probation, he would call for some exhibition of his skill. At night, however, instead of a commissioner came a messenger from him to bespeak a very large delivery of game for court, and to countermand the preparations for his own reception until that night.

On the receipt of this news, William was ready to sink to the ground; and his alarm would certainly have raised suspicions, had it not been ascribed to the delay of his marriage. He was now under the necessity of going out to hunt, and of sacrificing, at least, one of his balls. With the other he vowed to himself that he would not part for any purpose on earth, except for the final shot before the commissioner, which was to decide his fate for life.

Bertram scolded, when William came back from the forest with only a single buck: for the quantity of venison ordered was very considerable. Next day he was still more provoked on seeing Rudolph return loaded with game, and William with an empty bag. At night he threatened to dismiss him from his house, and revoke his consent to his marriage with Katharine, unless he brought home, at least, two roe-deer on the following morning. Katharine herself was in the greatest distress, and conjured him for love of her to apply his utmost zeal, and not to think so much about her whilst engaged in hunting.

In a despairing mood William set off for the forest. Kate, in any case, he looked upon as lost; and all that remained for him was a sad alternative between the two modes of losing her, whether by the result of this day's hunting, or of the trial before the commissioner. This was an alternative on which he felt himself incapable of deciding; and he was standing lost in gloomy contemplation of his wretched fate, when all at once a troop of deer advanced close upon him. Mechanically he felt for his last ball; it seemed to weigh a hundredweight in his hand. Already he had resolved to reserve this treasure at any price, when suddenly he saw the old wooden-leg at a distance, and apparently directing his steps towards himself. Joyfully he dropped his ball into the barrel, fired, and two roe-bucks fell to the ground. William left them lying, and hurried after the wooden-leg; but he had wholly disappeared. Father Bertram was well satisfied with William; but not so was William with himself. The whole day long he went about in gloomy despondency; the tenderness and caresses of Kate had no power to restore him to serenity. At night-fall, he was still buried in abstraction; and, seated in a chair, he hardly noticed the lively conversation between the forester and Rudolph, till at length the former awoke him out of his reverie.

'What, William, I say,' cried Bertram, 'sure you'll never sit by and hearken quietly whilst such scandalous things are said as Rudolph has just been saying of our forefather Kuno. I'll not sit and hear such things said of our Kuno. What, man? Kuno died in his bed quietly, and with a christian's peace, amongst his children and children's children; but the man that tampers with the powers of darkness never makes a good end. I know *that* by what I saw myself at Prague in Bohemia, when I was an apprentice lad.'

'Aye, what was that?' cried Rudolph and the rest: 'tell us, dear father.'

'What was it? why bad enough,' said Bertram, 'it makes me shudder when I think on it. There was, at that time, a young man in Prague one George Smith by name, a wild daring sort of fellow. And a very fair hunter he might have proved; but he was too hasty by far, and flung his shots away in a manner.

The Fatal Marksman

One day, when we had been joking him on this, his pride mounted so high, that nothing would serve him but he must defy all the hunters in a body: he would beat any of them at shooting: and no game should escape him, whether in the air or in the forest. This was his boast; but ill kept his word. Two days after comes a strange huntsman bolt upon us out of a thicket, and tells us that a little way off, on the main road, a man was lying half dead, and with nobody to look after him. We lads made up to the spot, and there, sure enough, lay poor George, torn and clawed all to pieces, just as if he had fallen amongst wild cats; not a word could he speak, for he was quite senseless, and hardly shewed any signs of life. We carried him to a house: one of us set off with the news to Prague; and thither he was soon fetched. Well, this George Smith, before he died, made confession that he had set about casting devil's balls, with an old upland hunter; devil's balls, you understand never miss; and because he failed in something that he should have done, the devil had handled him so roughly, that what must pay for it but his precious life?'

'But did George not relate what it was that brought such rough treatment upon him?'

'Aye, sure enough, before the magistrate he confessed all. As it drew towards midnight, it seems he had gone with the old hunter to a cross road: there they made a circle with a bloody sword; and in this circle they laid a skull and bones cross-ways. Then the old man told George what he was to do.

On the stroke of eleven, he was to begin casting the balls, in number sixty and three, neither more nor less; one over nor one under, as soon as twelve o'clock struck, he was a lost man. And during all this work, he was not to speak a word, nor to step out of the circle, let what would happen. Sixty of the balls were to carry true, and only three were to miss. Smith began casting the balls; but such shocking and hideous apparitions flocked about him, that at last he shrieked out, and jumped right out of the circle: instantly he fell down senseless to the ground, and never recovered his recollection till he found himself at Prague, in the hands of a surgeon, and with a clergyman by his side.'

'God preserve all Christian people from such snares of Satan,' said the forester's wife, crossing herself. The forester went to bed, and left William in the most wretched state of agitation. In vain he threw himself on the bed; sound sleep fled from his eyes. The delirium of a heated fancy presented to his eyes by turns, in confused groups, the old wooden-legged soldier, George, Katharine, and the ducal commissioner. Now the unfortunate boy of Prague held up his hand before him, as a bloody memento of warning; and then in a moment his threatening aspect would change into the face of Kate, fainting and pale as death; and near her stood the wooden-leg, his countenance overspread with a fiendish laugh of mockery. At another time he was standing before the commissioner in the act of firing his probationary shot; he levelled, took aim, fired, and – missed. Katharine fainted away, her father rejected him for ever; then came the wooden-leg, and presented him with fresh balls; but too late, no second trial was allowed him.

So passed the night with William. At the earliest dawn he went into the forest, and bent his steps, not altogether without design, to the spot where he had met the old soldier. The fresh breezy air of the morning had chased away from his mind the gloomy phantoms of the night. 'Fool!' said he to himself, 'because a mystery is above thy comprehension, must it therefore be from hell? And what is there so much out of the course of nature in that which I am seeking, that supernatural powers need to come to help me? Man controls the mighty powers of the brute into obedience to his will; why should he not, by the same natural arts, impress motion and direction upon the course of a bit of lifeless inert metal? Nature teems with operations which we do not comprehend; and am I to trifle away my happiness for a superannuated prejudice? I will call up no spiritual beings, but I will summon and make use of the occult powers of nature, never troubling myself whether I can decypher her mysteries or not. I shall go in quest of the old soldier; and, if I should not find him, I shall take care to keep up my courage better than that same George of Prague; he was surged on by pride, but I by the voice of love and honour.'

In this manner did William discuss his own intentions: but the old soldier was nowhere to be found. Nobody, of whom he inquired, had seen any such man as he had described. The next day was spent in the same search, and with it no better success.

'So be it then!' said William internally: 'the days that remain for my purpose are numbered. This very night will I go to the cross-road in the forest. It is a lonely spot; nobody will be there to witness my nocturnal labours: and I'll take care not to quit the circle till my work is done.' Twilight had set in; and William had provided himself with lead, bullet-mould, coals, and all other requisites, that he might be ready to slip out of the house unobserved immediately after supper. He was just on the point of departing, and had already wished the forester a good night, when the latter stopped him and took his hand.

'William,' said he, 'I know not what is come to me, but so it is, that this evening I have an awe upon my mind, as if from some danger, God knows what, hanging over me. Oblige me by staying this night with me. Don't look so cast down, my lad: it's only to guard against possibilities.'

William was at first disposed to excuse himself: but Kate commended her father so earnestly to his care, that her requests were not to be resisted; and he staid with a good grace, and put off the execution of his plan until the succeeding night.

A second night, and a second resolve, was in like manner broken through by the unexpected arrival of a dear uncle of

William's.

The third night came, and now whatever was to be done, must be done, for the next was the day of trial. From morning to night had old Anne, with her daughter Kate, busded about the house, to make arrangements for the suitable reception of her dignified guest, the commissioner; and at night-fall everything was ready. Anne embraced William on his return from the forest, and, for the first time, saluted him with the endearing name of son. The eyes of Kate sparkled with the tender emotions of a youthful bride, loving and beloved. The table was decked with festal flowers, and viands more luxurious than usual were brought out by the mother.

'This night,' said Bertram, 'we will keep the bridal feast: tomorrow we shall not be alone, and cannot, therefore, sit so confidentially and affectionately together; let us be happy then, as happy as if the pleasure of our lives were to be crowded into this one night.'

The forester embraced his family, and was deeply moved. 'But, Bertram,' said his wife, 'let us be as happy as we will tonight, I've a notion that the young people will be happier tomorrow. Do you know what I mean?'

'Yes, love, I know what you mean; and let the children know it also, that they may enjoy their happiness beforehand. Do you hear, children? The vicar is invited tomorrow, and as soon as William has passed his examination –'

At this moment a rusding noise and a loud cry from

Katharine interrupted the forester's speech. Kuno's portrait had again fallen from the wall, and a corner of the frame had wounded Katharine on the temples. The nail appeared to have been fixed too loosely in the wall, for it fell after the picture, and brought away part of the plaster. 'What, in God's name, can be the reason,' said Bertram with vexation, 'that this picture can't be made to hang as it should do? This is now the second time that it has alarmed us.'

William was thrown into dreadful agitation when he beheld the death-pale countenance of Kate, and the blood upon her temples. Just so had she appeared to him on the night of his hideous visions; and all the sad images of that memorable night now rushed upon his mind, and tormented him afresh. The violent shock tended greatly to stagger him in his plans for the night; but the wine, which he drank in large draughts, and more hastily than usual, for the purpose of hiding his anguish, filled him with a frantic spirit of hardihood: he resolved afresh to make the attempt boldly, and no longer saw anything in his purpose, but the honourable spectacle of love and courage struggling with danger.

The clock struck nine. William's heart beat violendy. He sought for some pretext for withdrawing, but in vain: what pretext could a man find for quitting his young bride on their bridal festival? Time flew faster than an arrow: in the arms of love, that should have crowned him with happiness, he suffered the pangs of martyrdom. Ten o'clock was now passed, and the decisive moment was at hand. Without taking leave, William stole from the side of his bride: already he was outside the house with his implements of labour, when old Anne came after him. 'Whither away, William, at this time of night?' asked she anxiously. 'I shot a deer, and forgot it in my hurry,' was the answer. In vain she begged him to stay; all her entreaties were flung away, and even the tender caresses of Kate, whose mind misgave her, that some mystery lay buried in his hurry and agitation. William tore himself from them both, and hastened to the forest.

The moon was in the wane, and, at this time was rising, and resting with a dim red orb upon the horizon. Gloomy clouds were flying over head, and at intervals darkened the whole country, which, by fits, the moon again lit up. The silvery birches and the aspen trees rose like apparitions in the forest; and the poplars seemed, to William's fevered vision, pale shadowy forms that beckoned him to retire. He shuddered; and it suddenly struck him, that the almost miraculous disturbance of his scheme on the two preceding nights, together with the repeated and ominous falling of the picture, were the last dissuasion from a wicked enterprise, addressed to him by his better angel that was now ready to forsake him.

Once again he faltered in his purpose. Already he was on the point of returning, when suddenly a voice appeared to whisper to him, 'Fool! hast thou not already accepted magical help? is it only for the trouble of reaping it, that thou wouldst forego the main harvest of its gifts?' He stood still. The moon issued in splendour from behind a dark cloud, and illuminated the peaceful roof of the forester's cottage. He could see Katharine's chamber window, glancing under the silvery rays: in the blindness of love, he stretched out his arm towards it, and mechanically stepped homewards. – Then came a second whisper from the voice for a sudden gust of wind brought the sound of the clock striking the half hour. 'Away to business!' it seemed to say. 'Right, right!' he said aloud, 'away to business! It is weak and childish to turn back from a business half accomplished; it is folly to renounce the main advantage, having already perhaps risked one's salvation for a trifle. No, let me go through with it.'

He stepped forwards with long strides: the wind drove the agitated clouds again over the face of the moon, and William plunged into the thickest gloom of the forest.

At length he stood upon the cross-way. At length the magic circle was drawn; the skulls were fixed, and the bones were laid round about. The moon buried itself deeper and deeper in the clouds; and no light was shed upon the midnight deed, except from the red lurid gleam of the fire, that waxed and waned by fits, under the gusty squalls of the wind. A remote church-clock proclaimed that it was now within a quarter of eleven. William put the ladle upon the fire, and threw in the lead, together with three bullets, which had already hit the mark once: a practice, amongst those who cast the 'fatal bullets', which he remembered to have heard in his apprenticeship. In the forest was now heard a pattering of rain. At intervals came flitting motions of owls, bats, and other light-shunning creatures, scared by the sudden gleams of the fire: some, dropping from the surrounding boughs, placed themselves on the magic circle, where, by their low dull croaking, they seemed to be holding dialogues, in some unknown tongue, with the dead men's skulls. Their numbers increased; and, amongst them were indistinct outlines of misty forms, that went and came, some with brutal, some with human faces. Their vapoury lineaments fluctuated and obeyed the motions of the wind: one only stood unchanged, and like a shadow near to the circle; and setded the sad light of its eyes steadfastly upon William. Sometimes it would raise its pale hands, and seem to sigh: and when it raised its hands, the fire would burn more sullenly; but a grey owl would then fan with his wings and rekindle the decaying embers. William averted his eyes: for the countenance of his buried mother seemed to look out for the cloudy figure, with piteous expressions of unutterable anguish. Suddenly it struck eleven; and then the shadow vanished, with the action of one whp prays and breathes up sighs to heaven. The owls and the night-ravens flitted croaking about; and the skulls and bones rattled beneath their wings. William kneeled down on his coaly hearth: and with the last stroke of eleven, out fell the first bullet.

The owls, and the bones, were now silent. But along the

road came an old crooked beldame pell-mell against the magic circle. She was hung round with wooden spoons, ladles, and other kitchen utensils; and made a hideous rattling as she moved. The owls saluted her with hooting, and stroked her with their wings. At the circle, she bowed to the bones and skulls; but the coals shot forth lambent tongues of flame against her, and she drew back her withered hands. Then she paced round the circle, and with a grin presented her wares to William. 'Give me the spoons.'

> Give the skulls to me, love:
> What's the trumpery to thee, love:

And then she chaunted, with a scornful air,

> There's nothing can help: 'tis an hour too late;
> Nothing can step betwixt thee and thy fate.
> Shoot in the light, or shoot in the dark,
> Thy bullets, be sure, shall go true to the mark.
> 'Shoot the dove,' says the word of command;
> And the forester bold, with 'the skilful hand'
> Levels and fires: oh! marksman good!
> The dove lies bathed in its innocent blood!
> Here's to the man that shoots the dove!
> Come for the prize to me, my love!

William was aghast with horror: but he remained quiet

within the circle, and pursued his labours. The old woman was one whom he knew well. A crazy old female beggar had formerly roamed about the neighbourhood in this attire; till at last she was lodged in a mad-house. He was at a loss to discover, whether the object now before him were the reality or an illusion. After some little pause, the old crone scattered her lumber to the right and left with an angry air, and then tottered slowly away into the gloomy depths of the forest, singing these words:

> This is to the left, and that to the right:
> This and that for the bridal-night.
> Marksman fine, be sure and steady,
> The bride she is dressed – the priest he is ready,
> Tomorrow, tomorrow, when day-light departs,
> And twilight is spread over broken hearts,
> When the fight is fought, when the race is run,
> When the strife and the anguish are over and done;
> When the bridal-bed is decked with a winding-sheet,
> Then comes a bridegroom for me, I trow,
> That shall live with me in my house of woe.
> Here's to him that shoots the dove!
> Come for the prize to me, my love!

Now came all at once a rattling as of wheels, and the cracking of postillions' whips. A carriage and six drove up with outriders. 'What the devil's this that stops the way?' cried the man who rode the leaders. 'Make way there, I say, clear the road.' William looked up, and saw sparks of fire darting from the horses' hoofs, and a circle of flame about the carriage-wheels. By this he knew it to be a work of the fiend, and never stirred. 'Push on, my lads, drive over him, helter-skelter,' cried the same postillion, looking back to the others; and in a moment the whole equipage moved rapidly upon the circle. William cowered down to the ground, beneath the dash of the leader's fore legs; but the airy train, and the carriage, soared into the air with a whistling sound, round and round the circle, and vanished in a hurricane, which moved not a leaf of the trees. Some time elapsed before William recovered from his consternation. However, he compelled his trembling hands to keep firm, and cast a few bullets. At that moment, a well-known church clock at a distance, began to strike. At first the sound was a sound of comfort, connecting, as with the tones of some friendly voice, the human world with the dismal circle in which he stood, that else seemed cut off from it as by an impassable gulph: but the clock struck twice, thrice, – here he shuddered at the rapid flight of time, for his work was not a third part advanced, then it struck a fourth time. He was appalled; every limb seemed palsied; and the mould slipped out of his nerveless hand. With the calmness of despair, he listened to the clock, until it completed the full hour of twelve; the knell then vibrated on the air, lingered, and died away. To sport with the solemn hour of midnight, appeared too bold an undertaking, even for the powers of darkness. However, he drew out his watch, looked, and behold! it was no more than half past eleven.

Recovering his courage, and now fully steeled against all fresh illusions, he resumed his labours with energy. Profound quiet was all around him, – disturbed only at intervals by the owls that made a low muttering, and now and then rattled the skulls and bones together. All at once a crashing was heard in the bushes. The sound was familiar to the experienced hunter's ears; he looked around; and as he expected, a wild boar sprang out and rushed up to the circle. 'This,' thought William, 'is no deception;' and he leaped up, seized his gun, and snapped it hastily at the wild beast; but no spark issued from the flint: he drew his hanger; but the brisdy monster, like the carriage and horses, soared far above him into the air and vanished.

William, thus repeatedly baffled, now hastened to bring up the lost time. Sixty bullets were already cast: he looked upland suddenly the clouds opened, and the moon again threw a brilliant light over the whole country. Just then a voice was heard from the depths of the forest, crying out, in great agitation, 'William! William!' It was the voice of Kate. William saw her issue from the bushes, and fearfully look round her. Behind her panted the old woman, stretching her withered spidery arms after the flying girl, and endeavouring to catch hold of her floating garments. Katharine now collected the last remains of her exhausted strength for flight: at that moment, the old wooden-leg stepped across her path; for an instant it checked her speed, and then the old hag caught her with her bony hands. William could contain himself no longer: he threw the mould with the last bullet out of his hands, and would have leaped out of the circle: but just then the clock struck twelve; the fiendish vision had vanished; the owls threw the skulls and bones confusedly together, and flew away; the fire went out; and William sunk exhausted to the ground.

Now came up slowly a horseman upon a black horse. He stopped at the effaced outline of the magic circle, and spoke thus: 'Thou hast stood thy trial well: what would'st thou have of me?'

'Nothing of thee, nothing at all,' said William, 'what I want – I have prepared for myself.'

'Aye; but with my help: therefore part belongs to me.'

'By no means, by no means: I bargained for no help; I summoned thee not.'

The horseman laughed scornfully; 'Thou art bolder,' said he, 'than such as thou are wont to be. Take the balls which thou hast cast!

> Sixty for thee, three for me:
> The sixty go true, the three go askew:
> All will be plain, when we meet again.'

William averted his face: 'I will never meet thee again,' said he, – 'leave me.'

'Why turnest thou away?' said the stranger, with a dreadful laugh: 'dost know me?'

'No, no,' said William, shuddering: 'I know thee not! I wish not to know thee. Be thou who thou mayest, leave me!'

The Black Horseman turned away his horse, and said with a gloomy solemnity of voice. 'Thou *dost* know me: the very hair of thy head, which stands on end, confesses for thee that thou dost. I am he – whom at this moment thou namest in thy heart with horror.' So saying, he vanished, followed by the dreary sound of withered leaves, and the echo of blasted boughs falling from the trees beneath which he had stood.

'Merciful God! what has happened to you, William?' exclaimed Katharine and her mother, as William returned, pale and agitated after midnight, 'you look as if fresh risen from the grave.'

'Nothing, nothing,' said William, 'nothing but the night air; – the truth is, I am a little feverish.'

'William, William!' said old Bertram, 'you cannot deceive me: something has met you in the forest. Why would you not stop at home? Something has crossed your on the road, I'll swear.'

William was struck with the old man's seriousness, and replied, 'Well, yes; I acknowledge something has crossed me; but wait for nine days: before then, you know yourself that –'

'Gladly, gladly son,' said Bertram, 'and God be praised, that it is anything of that kind that can wait for nine days. Trouble him not wife; Kate, leave him at peace I now my good lad, go to bed, and rest thyself. "Night," says the proverb, "is no man's friend." But be of good cheer: the man that is in his vocation, and walks only in lawful paths, may bid defiance to the fiends of darkness, and all their works.'

William needed his utmost powers of dissimulation to disguise from the old man's penetration how little his suspicions had done him injustice. This indulgent affection of Father Bertram, and such unshaken confidence in his uprightness wrung his heart. He hurried to his bedroom, with full determination to destroy the accursed bullets.

'One only will I keep, only one will I use,' said he, holding out his supplicating hands pressed palm to palm, with bitter tears towards heaven. 'Oh let the purpose, let the purpose, plead for the offence; plead for me the anguish of my heart, and the trial which I could not bear! I will humble, I will abase myself in the sight of God: with a thousand, with ten thousand penitential acts I will wash out the guilt of my transgression. But can I, can I now go back, without making shipwreck of all things – of my happiness, of my honour, my darling Katharine?'

Somewhat tranquillized by this view of his own conduct, he beheld the morning dawn with more calmness than he had anticipated.

The ducal commissioner arrived, and expressed a wish previous to the decisive trial, of making a little hunting excursion in company with the young forester. 'For,' said he, 'between ourselves, the hunter's skill is best shewn in the forest.'

William turned pale, and would have made excuses, but as these availed nothing with the commissioner, he begged at least that he might be allowed to stand his trial first. Old Bertram shook his head thoughtfully. 'William, William,' said he, with a deep tremulous tone. William withdrew instantly, and in a few moments he was equipped for the chase, and with Bertram followed the commissioner into the forest.

The old forester sought to suppress his misgivings, but struggled in vain to assume a cheerful aspect. Katharine was dejected and agitated, and went about her household labours as if dreaming, 'Was it not possible,' she asked her father, 'to put off the trial?' – 'I thought of that also,' replied he, and he kissed her in silence. Recovering himself immediately, he congratulated his daughter on the day – and reminded her of her bridal garland.

The garland had been locked up by old Anne in the drawer; and hastily attempting to open it she injured the lock. A child was therefore dispatched to a shop to fetch another garland for the bride. 'Bring the handsomest they have,' cried dame Anne after the child; but the child, in its simplicity, pitched upon that which glittered most; and this happened to be a bride's funeral garland of myrtle and rosemary entwined with silver, which the mistress of the shop, not knowing the circumstances, allowed the child to carry off. The bride and her mother well understood the ominous import of this accident! each shuddered; and flinging her arms about the other's neck, sought to stifle her horror in a laugh at the child's blunder. The lock was now tried once more; it opened readily; the coronals were exchanged; and the beautiful tresses of Katharine were enwreathed with the blooming garland of a bride.

The hunting party returned. The Commissioner was inexhaustible in William's praise. 'After such proofs of skill,' said he, 'it seems ridiculous that I should call for any other test; but to satisfy old ordinances we are sometimes obliged to do more than is absolutely needful; and so we will dispatch the matter as briefly as possible. Yonder is a dove sitting on that pillar: level and bring her down.'

'Oh! not *that*, not *that*, for God's sake, William,' cried Katharine, hastening to the spot; 'shoot not for God's sake at the dove. Ah! William, last night I dreamed that I was a white dove; and my mother put a ring about my neck; then came you, and in a moment my mother was covered with blood.'

William drew back his piece which he had already levelled; but the Commissioner laughed – 'Eh! what!' said he, 'so timorous? That will never do for a forester's wife: courage, young bride, courage! – Or stay, may be the dove is a pet dove of your own?'

'No,' said Katharine, 'but the dream has sadly sunk my spirits' – 'Well, then,' said the Commissioner, 'if that's all, pluck 'em up again and so fire away, Mr Forester.'

He fired; and at the same instant, with a piercing shriek, fell Katharine to the ground.

'Strange girl!' said the Commissioner, fancying that she had fallen only from panic, and raised her up, but a stream of blood flowed down her face; her forehead was shattered; and a bullet lay sunk in the wound.

'What is the matter?' exclaimed William, as the cry resounded behind him. He turned and saw Katharine with a deadly paleness lying stretched in her blood. By her side stood the old wooden-leg, in a fiendish mockery, and snarling out –

'Sixty go true.

Three go askew.'

In the madness of his wrath, William drew his hanger, and made a thrust at the hideous creature. 'Accursed devil!' cried he in tones of despair – 'Is it thus thou hast deluded me?' More he had no power to utter; for he sank insensible on the ground close by his bleeding bride.

The commissioner and the priest sought vainly to speak comforts to the desolate parents. Scarce had the aged mother laid the ominous funeral garland upon the bosom of her daughter's corpse, when she swept away the last tears of her unfathomable grief. The solitary father soon followed her. William, the Fatal Marksman, wore away his days in a madhouse.